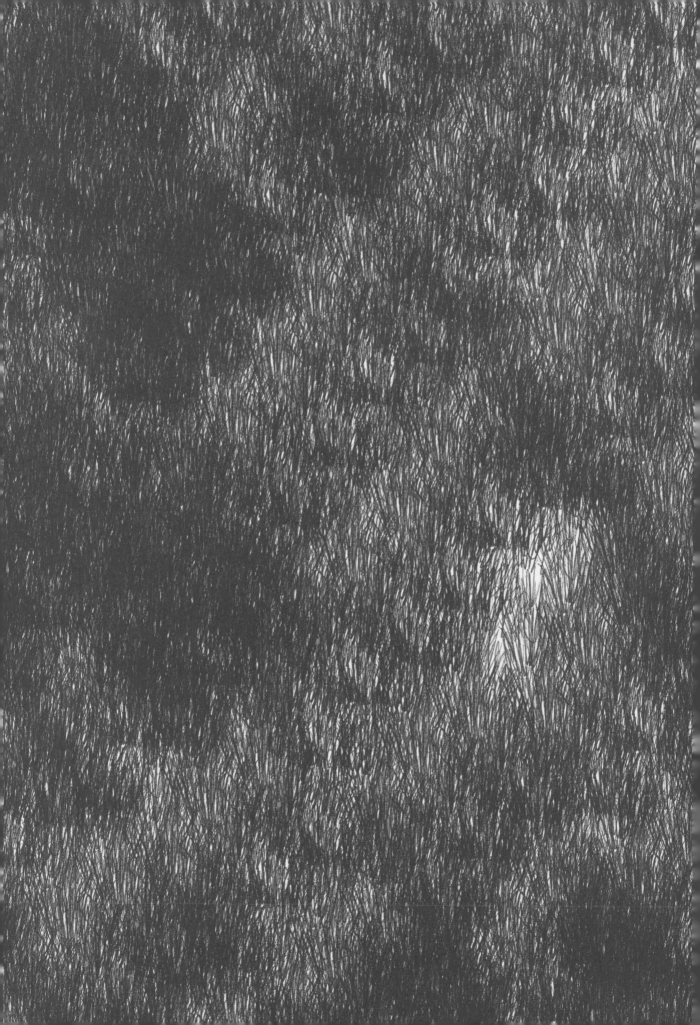

TOON TELLEGEN – MARC BOUTAVANT

The Day
No One
Was Angry

GECKO PRESS

THE HYRAX

Every evening at sunset, the hyrax climbed a small hill. "Don't set!" he yelled. "Just this once, don't do it. I'm telling you!"

He shook his fists, jumped up and down, and was so cross he got tears in his eyes. But, every time, the sun went down.

When the last slice of the sun had sunk beneath the horizon, the hyrax dried his tears, shook his head, and went home, disappointed.

The hyrax lived in a small, dark house in the middle of the grasslands. He knew nobody and nobody knew him.

Back home, he would lie on his bed with his hands behind his head and wonder why the sun never listened to him. Surely it could stay up just once, he would think to himself. That's not too much to ask, is it? Maybe I should get more angry. Threaten him with something. A kick, perhaps. Or I could tell him I'm going away so there'll be no one for him to shine on.

Every night, the hyrax thought about the sun for hours. He wished he could go to the horizon to hold up the sun with his bare hands. Or build a kind of platform, perhaps, so it couldn't sink any further. But he feared the sun was too big and too strong for him.

The sun is a trickster, he decided. He shines all day long so you think he'll shine forever, and then suddenly, down he goes. That's trickery.

The hyrax could never fall asleep until late at night.

Each morning when he woke, the sun was already up and shining, and the hyrax would think scornfully, Yes, yes, I know—you're not even sorry. This is just what you do.

He would put on a wide hat so he didn't have to see the sun and make his way outside.

But each evening, he would climb the hill again and yell, "There you are! Going down again! Why don't you just stay put for once!" Then back home he would go, without achieving a thing.

That's how life was for the hyrax, screaming until he was hoarse, and stamping his feet till he was exhausted.

Every evening he stood on his hill, staring reproachfully at the sun. He knows what I want him to do, he would think. He knows he'd only have to do it once to make me happy. Just one time in a million . . . that's not much to ask. But he takes no notice.

The hyrax shook his head. But really, he thought, does anyone ever listen?

All about him, the grasslands stretched away; the sky hung wide and empty overhead, and in the distance, the last of the sun slipped beneath the horizon.

As far as the hyrax was concerned, nothing ever listened.

THE ELEPHANT

"Don't climb," the elephant said to himself as he stood under the poplar tree one afternoon. He already had big bumps all over his head, his back, and his trunk.

He put one foot on the lowest branch.

"What did I tell you?" he scolded.

"Don't climb," he said in a low voice.

"And what are you doing?"

"I'm climbing."

"Put your foot down!"

"No," he murmured, lowering his eyes.

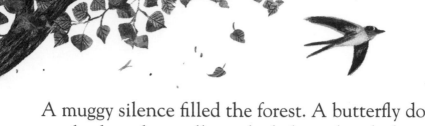

A muggy silence filled the forest. A butterfly dozed in a rose bush and a swallow whirled overhead, skimming the trees.

The elephant put his other feet on the lowest branch of the poplar tree.

"Now you're making me really cross," he said. "Get down!"

He didn't answer.

"Get down! You heard me, didn't you? How many bumps do you have already? How many more do you want? Do you want to break something?"

"No," he whispered. "I don't want to break anything."

"Well, your brain's already cracked," he said sarcastically.

"Ah, my brain," he said, shrugging his shoulders. "I'm not climbing with my brain."

He climbed onto the next branch then whacked himself with his trunk, once, twice.

"You aren't listening!" he trumpeted. "Get down!"

"I am listening," he said. "I'm just not taking any notice of you. I want to climb."

"Climb, climb . . ." He was so angry his voice came out in a croak.

Slowly, he climbed higher.

Then he gave a great, despairing sigh. "A lost cause," he said.

"What's a lost cause?" he asked.

"You," he said. "You're a lost cause."

"I'm halfway there," he said.

He kept quiet, merely shaking his head.
Then he looked up.
"The top!" he cried. "I'm almost there!"
He reached the top of the tree and looked all around
him. The forest stretched away at his feet and, in the
distance, the sun bounced off the waves. He had never
seen anything so beautiful.
He stood on one leg, flapped his ears, lifted his trunk,
and attempted a pirouette in sheer delight.

But he tripped.

And he fell, crashing through the branches of the poplar tree.

Right now I could be thinking I told you so, he thought as he fell. But that's not how I see it. Not at all. No. He gritted his teeth. I'll never see it that way.

What was it I am exactly? he wondered as he fell through the last branches. Oh, yes, I'm a lost cause.

Then he hit the ground, making an elephant-sized crater, and he no longer knew what or where he was. An enormous bump was swelling on the back of his head, and poplar leaves and branches rained down on him.

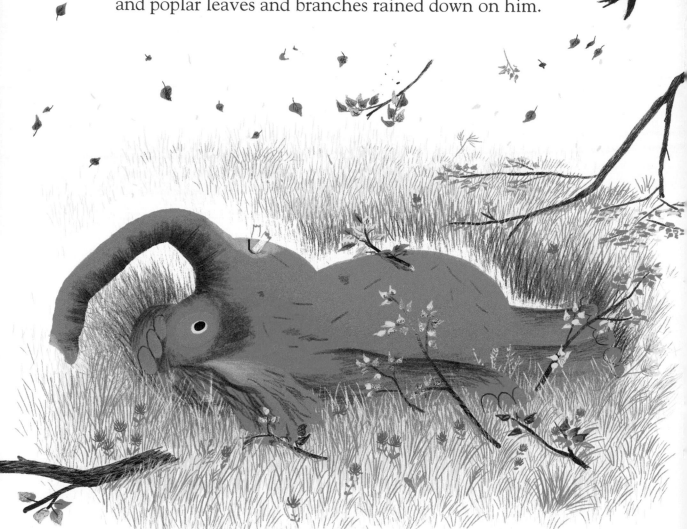

THE EARTHWORM
AND THE BEETLE

"I'm very angry," said the beetle, one winter's evening.

"Well, I'm even angrier," said the earthworm.

They were sitting side by side in the twilight, under the rose bush.

"You can't be!" said the beetle. "You're not angrier than I am."

"No?" cried the earthworm.

"No!" yelled the beetle.

They sprang up, ten times more angry than before. Their heads and shoulders turned red with anger and soon they were surrounded by animals who couldn't believe their eyes.

"Goodness, they are angry," they said.

"I'm much angrier than he is!" yelled the beetle.

"No! I am!" yelled the earthworm.

The animals circled the beetle and the earthworm.
They cautiously touched their red-hot shoulders,
scorching their paws and feathers, shaking their
heads and discussing what to do.

It took them a good while to agree, but at last they
said, "You're both very angry. But the angriest one is . . .
the beetle."

"Ha-ha!" said the beetle. "I knew it!" He grinned and
bowed to everyone.

The earthworm began to rant and rave even more
fiercely.

"I'm angrier!" he screamed. "I am!"

The animals cowered, and a couple fell over
backwards. The earthworm's eyes flashed with sparks.

The grass caught fire. And the earthworm's anger blazed ever hotter.

When the beetle saw this, he thought: Now *that's* angry. He scratched behind his ear. But I'm angrier than he is. Didn't they say so?

He cleared his throat and began to screech with anger, louder than a beetle had ever screeched before.

The other animals melted into the background, then they ran away as fast as they could.

"Yes," they agreed, frightened, "the beetle is definitely angrier."

"Yes!" screeched the beetle, no longer grinning.

Stamping and screeching, the beetle and the earthworm stood side by side in the middle of the forest.

Night fell. Tufts of mist drifted up between the bushes. The moon appeared. It was many hours before the beetle and the earthworm stopped being angry.

Then the beetle and the earthworm brushed off each other's shoulders and shared a friendly slap or two.

"You were really angry, earthworm," said the beetle.

"But you were even angrier," said the earthworm.

"Ah, well," said the beetle, bashfully.

Soon after, they went to the earthworm's house for a bite to eat. The moon shone down, and now and then a branch creaked in a tree or in the misty bushes. The night was calm.

THE SQUIRREL
AND THE AARDVARK

One afternoon, the squirrel was strolling through the
bushes not far from the river.

"Squirrel!" he heard someone call.

The squirrel looked around. At first, he saw nothing.
Then he noticed two legs waving, or thrashing about—he
couldn't quite tell which.

"Who's that?" he asked.

"It's me," said the voice. "Aardvark. Hi there! Ha-ha!"

Parting the bushes, the squirrel could see the aardvark.
He was standing on his head, laughing.

Surprised, the squirrel came to a standstill.

"Why are you on your head?" he asked.

"Because it's fun, of course!" said the aardvark.
He carried on laughing and waving his legs. "But it's not
only for fun, if that's what you're thinking."

"No," said the squirrel. "But if you stood on your legs . . ."

"Then I'd be angry," the aardvark cut in, almost choking with laughter. "Oh, squirrel, you can't imagine how angry I'd be . . ."

"Always?" asked the squirrel.

"Always," replied the aardvark. "Help me stand up," he said, trying to give the squirrel a friendly nod.

The squirrel hesitated, even though it was hard to believe that standing up really would make the aardvark angry.

He grasped him around the waist and turned him over.

At once, the aardvark began to howl and his eyes flashed fire.

"You see!" he yelled furiously. "See! Loathsome squirrel."

The squirrel leaped back as the aardvark rushed at him, trying to run him down.

"I see," the squirrel murmured.

A struggle ensued. The aardvark hit the squirrel, but in his fury he hit himself even harder. He rained curses on the squirrel.

With great difficulty, the squirrel succeeded in grabbing the aardvark by the hind legs and standing him back on his head.

"Ha-ha!" chortled the aardvark. "That was so funny! Hilarious! You saw how angry I was?"

The squirrel sat a while on the ground, breathing hard, unable to utter a word. The aardvark waved his legs about and cried: "It's so awful being angry, isn't it, squirrel? The happier we are, the better!"

The squirrel stood up, brushing off his shoulders and tail.

"Do you have to stay in that position all the time?" he asked.

"Always," the aardvark laughed. "But do I *have* to? No, I *want* to."

The squirrel was silent.

"Because if I don't," said the aardvark, drumming on his stomach with such hilarity that he almost fell over, "the consequences are incalculable."

The squirrel decided to go on his way, and he bid the aardvark farewell.

"Ha-ha!" said the aardvark. "You're going already?"

"Yes," replied the squirrel.

With great dignity, the squirrel left the bushes and headed for the river.

"*Incalculable*," he heard the aardvark bellow with laughter. "The consequences are incalculable!"

The squirrel heard a thump as if someone had fallen over, and he quickened his pace.

THE LOBSTER

The lobster knocked at the mouse's door.

"Yes?" said the mouse.

The lobster went inside. He carried a suitcase which he put on the table.

"I'm the lobster," he said. "Can I interest you in some anger?"

"Anger?" asked the mouse, who knew the lobster well.

"Yes," said the lobster crustily. "Anger. You want to get angry now and then, don't you?"

"Yes," said the mouse, "but if I want to get angry, I do—just like that. It happens all by itself."

"But is it always the right kind of anger?" asked the lobster, looking keenly at the mouse.

The mouse hesitated.

"As I thought," said the lobster. "Not the right kind." He opened his suitcase. "I'll show you what I have."

The suitcase was dark inside. The lobster took out an assortment of angers, one by one.

"Does anyone ever step on your toes while you're dancing?" he asked.

"Yes," said the mouse.

"For that I have a mild anger, which leaves as quickly as it arrives," said the lobster, showing him a thin, light-red anger. "Rather pretty," he added.

Then, glancing at the mouse, he asked, "Have you ever forgotten to pack something when you've gone away?"

"Yes, often," replied the mouse. "How did you know?"

"I have just the thing for that," said the lobster.

A gray, wrinkled irritation billowed from the suitcase.

The mouse nodded. It was exactly the sort of anger that went with forgetting something.

"I already have one like that," he said.

The lobster showed him a purple rage, a green-tinted jealousy, and a white fury.

Right at the bottom of the suitcase, the mouse saw something light blue.

31

"What's that?" he asked.

"That's not anger." The lobster coughed. "It's sorrow. And not for sale. But seeing as it's you . . ."

"I'll take it," said the mouse.

"To tell the truth, it's actually melancholy," said the lobster, "which is deeper than sorrow."

He handed the mouse the light blue, transparent melancholy, closed the suitcase, and took himself off.

The mouse went and sat by his window. He draped the melancholy over his shoulders and stared into the distance.

It was a warm morning in early summer, with not a breath of wind.

"Ah . . ." said the mouse, sighing deeply.

THE HEDGEHOG

The hedgehog was sitting under the rose bush, thinking of all the things he'd been.

I've been joyful, he thought. On the squirrel's birthday, for instance, when I danced with the cricket. And I've been sad. That time the wind blew so hard it tore out all my quills—that time, I was really sad. And I've been content. Right now, I'm content.

He nodded and looked around. It was summer, he was content, and he was thinking. Thinking was what he liked doing best. Thinking about anything or nothing, nobody or everybody; it didn't matter.

But have I ever been angry? he wondered. He thought hard, but he couldn't remember ever being angry.

It might be about time, he decided. He badly wanted to be everything, even if it was only once.

It was late in the afternoon. The hedgehog closed his eyes and wondered: How does one become angry, exactly? He didn't know.

He had seen angry animals. He'd seen them stamping their feet and foaming at the mouth; he'd seen them biting, clawing, hitting; he'd heard them roaring and bellowing. But he knew that he couldn't do any of those things.

He screwed up his eyes. I've done that before, he thought. He scratched the prickles behind his ear. That too, he thought.

It was nearly evening when he realized that he might never be angry. That's sad, he thought.

Suddenly an idea came to him. You know what? he told himself. If I write it down, I'll be it. Because when I write, "I'm content," I am content. Otherwise I wouldn't write it. When I sign a letter, "The hedgehog," I am the hedgehog. He nodded to himself. I am what I write.

He found a piece of birch bark and on it he wrote,
"I am angry."

He read the words and shook his head in amazement.
Well, well. So now I'm angry, he thought. How strange. He
tried to feel exactly what he was feeling, rereading the words
two or three times, shaking his head.

This is the strangest feeling I've ever had, he thought. It's
not like anything else. But he was very pleased to be angry
at last.

So now I'm both angry and happy, he thought. And
amazed as well. That means I'm a lot of different things
all at once.

Just then a gust of wind snatched the bark from
his hand.

"Hey!" cried the hedgehog. "Give that back!
It's not a real letter!"

He didn't want anyone to read what he'd written.

If anyone finds out I'm angry, he thought, then . . . then . . . He didn't know what would happen, but he felt sure it would be terrible.

The wind gusted and blustered and took no notice. It thought the piece of birch bark was a real letter and carried it off into the air. It had no address and no sender. For ages, the wind whirled it about, high above the forest. Finally it tore the bark up and let the pieces flutter to the ground.

The hedgehog went on thinking in the twilight, under the rose bush. So, now I can say I've been angry, he thought. But have I ever been careless? He closed his eyes. Maybe that's what I am now . . . maybe reckless, even.

Night fell. Feeling content—which he liked best of all—the hedgehog rolled himself into a ball and took a rest from thinking.

THE SHREW

Very early one morning, the shrew knocked on the squirrel's door.

"Yes?" said the squirrel.

"Squirrel," said the shrew, "I hope you won't be angry. It's me, the shrew."

"I'm still in bed," said the squirrel.

"Does that mean you're angry?" asked the shrew.

"No," said the squirrel.

"So you won't be angry if I come inside?" asked the shrew.

"No," said the squirrel.

The shrew came inside and the squirrel got out of bed.

"It was my birthday yesterday," he said, yawning.

"I know," said the shrew. "That's why I've come today. I haven't brought a present, though. That will make you angry, won't it?"

"Not at all," said the squirrel. "Would you like a piece of cake? I still have half a chestnut cake."

The shrew sat at the table and tasted the cake the squirrel put in front of him.

"Squirrel," he said, after two bites, "I think this really will make you angry, but I have to tell you: I don't like this cake. Yuck! It's horrible." He pushed the cake away with a shudder. "That must make you angry!"

"Everyone else liked it," said the squirrel. He gathered up the leftovers, sniffed them, and nodded.

"I think," said the shrew, "that everyone hated it. Actually, none of them had ever tasted such a horrible cake but they were trying really hard not to show it. Out of politeness, squirrel. Only out of politeness." He wagged a finger and looked earnestly at the squirrel.

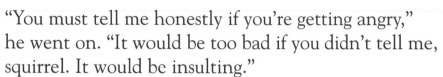

"You must tell me honestly if you're getting angry,"
he went on. "It would be too bad if you didn't tell me,
squirrel. It would be insulting."

But the squirrel shook his head. He wasn't angry and
he sat back at the table. He didn't know what insulting
meant.

The shrew looked down and his shoulders slumped.

They sat silently, face to face. The shrew scratched
the table, and now and then he cleared his throat. "Do
you mind if I say something else?" he asked.

"Go ahead," said the squirrel.

"I don't like it here," said the shrew. "Not one little
bit. And I'm not even sitting comfortably. That must
make you angry."

"I'm not angry," said the squirrel.

"You are!" cried the shrew, leaping onto the table.
"You're terribly angry. Pretending you're not won't
help! It never does!"

"I'm not angry," said the squirrel.

The shrew darted from one end of the table to the other, swung the lamp so it hit the ceiling and broke, stepped on a plate and two cups, kicked the broken pieces onto the floor, and yelled: "You are! You are! You are!" He tried to screech, but he didn't have the voice for it.

Meanwhile, the squirrel leaned back in his chair, remembering all the animals at his birthday party, recalling how they had danced and eaten and told him how much they were enjoying themselves, and how they hadn't gone home until late, the ant being the last to leave.

The shrew lost his footing, stumbled, and fell headfirst among the fragments of lamp, plate, and cups. He had a lump on his head and a bloody nose but he didn't utter a sound.

He stood up, dusted himself off, and said: "I'm going now."

"That's a pity," said the squirrel.

"A pity?" The shrew tried to read the squirrel's eyes. "Does that mean you're angry? Should I stay?"

The squirrel thought for a moment and then said slowly: "I—am—not—an—gry."

"Then I really am going," said the shrew, gloomily.

He went out. Halfway along the beech branch, he turned round. His forehead and nose were blue and swollen.

"I doubt if I'll ever come back, squirrel," he said.

"Oh," said the squirrel.

After a silence, the shrew said, "Are you happy now?"

The squirrel stood by his door, thinking long and hard.

"No," he finally replied.

The shrew sighed, and without another word he climbed down the beech tree and vanished into the forest.

THE HIPPOPOTAMUS
AND
THE RHINOCEROS

Right in the middle of the forest, the hippopotamus and the rhinoceros found themselves nose to nose.

The path was narrow and they couldn't get past each other.

"I'm not budging," said the hippopotamus.

"Me neither," said the rhinoceros.

They stared at one another.

"What now then?" asked the hippopotamus.

"What indeed," replied the rhinoceros.

It was the middle of the day. The sun shone through the leaves while the river chattered in the distance.

"Let's sit down," said the hippopotamus.

"All right," said the rhinoceros.

They sat down on the path and thought about it.

"Whatever happens, I'm not budging," the hippopotamus said, once or twice. "Just so you know."

"Me neither," said the rhinoceros. "Just so you know."

"We could get angry," said the hippopotamus after a long silence, "and charge at one another."

"We could," said the rhinoceros.

"Then one of us would have to move. We'd have no choice."

"That's right."

"But it certainly wouldn't be me," said the hippopotamus. He stood up and tried to look as formidable as possible.

"So you think it would be me?" said the rhinoceros, standing up in turn, threateningly.

"No." The hippopotamus sighed and sat back down. A long silence followed.

"Would you like some sweet grass?" he asked.

"Most certainly," said the rhinoceros.

The hippopotamus happened to have a pot of it with him. They ate it together. Then they told each other where they were going.

"But neither of us will budge," said the hippopotamus.

"No, never," said the rhinoceros.

They gave each other a few friendly pats on the shoulders and even did a few dance steps on the narrow path, right there in the middle of the forest. But they didn't pass each other. They made quite sure of that.

"We dance quite nicely together," said the hippopotamus.

"With feeling," said the rhinoceros.

"Yes, with feeling," the hippopotamus agreed.

When night fell, it was time to go home.

"Goodbye, hippopotamus," said the rhinoceros.

"Goodbye, rhinoceros," said the hippopotamus.

They turned round.

"But if I meet you again, I won't budge," said the hippopotamus.

"Me neither," cried the rhinoceros. "I guarantee it!"

They each went their own way home, trying to whistle through their teeth. Every now and then they retraced the dance steps they had made together in the middle of the narrow path, on their own.

THE ANT AND THE SQUIRREL

"If I told you I was going away on a trip," the ant asked the squirrel, "would you be sad?"

They were sitting on the riverbank, gazing across to the other side. It was summer, the sun was high overhead, and the river sparkled.

"Yes, I'd be sad," said the squirrel. "But if I said you couldn't go, would you be angry?"

"Yes, I'd be angry," said the ant. "But if I said I was going anyway and you couldn't stop me, would you be very sad?"

"Yes," said the squirrel, "I'd be very sad." He leaned back and closed his eyes. "But if I found a reason why you wouldn't want to go, would you be very angry?"

"What reason?" asked the ant.

"Ah . . ." said the squirrel. "I'll tell you when you've told me . . ."

"I want to know now!" cried the ant.

"But I haven't found the reason yet," said the squirrel.

"Then I'm going now," said the ant.

The squirrel felt sad and said, "You can't go."

The ant became angry. "I'm going anyway," he said. He took a step.

The squirrel sighed, slumping a little.

Nothing happened for a while.

"Well?" said the ant. "Have you found the reason?"

The squirrel shook his head. "You haven't gone yet."

"But I really am going," said the ant. He went a little way. Every couple of steps, he turned around.

"Well?" he asked each time. "Have you thought of it?"

Each time, the squirrel shook his head. It was very hard for him. He thought the ant might suddenly start running and keep going until he was so far away that he could never find his way back.

But he said nothing.

The ant kept going further and further until he was very small. His voice came in snatches: ". . . found . . . uirrel . . ."

Finally the squirrel lost sight of him.

Now he's really gone, he thought. He's gone for good. His eyes stung. Tears, he realized.

But, suddenly, a little cloud of dust appeared on the horizon. The ant came running back at top speed.

Moments later, he was back in front of the squirrel.

"Now you have to tell me," he said breathlessly.

He looked the squirrel right in the eyes and wagged a finger in his face. The dust cloud slowly settled.

I'll have to find something to tell him now, thought the squirrel, and he made something up.

THE TOAD

The toad was angry, so the ant suggested some things he could do about it.

He could simply blow his anger away, like dust. The ant blew some imaginary anger from his shoulder.

He could break it into pieces and crush it.

He could bury it and cover it with a boulder.

"A boulder?" asked the toad. "Where would I find one? And anyway, I'm no good at lifting."

"A small boulder would do," said the ant.

"A very small boulder," grumbled the toad.

"It is possible to forget about anger," the ant continued. "Or to build a wall around it."

"It would have to be a high wall, ant," said the toad. "Impossible to climb."

"Or leap over," said the ant.

"Or leap over," agreed the toad.

The toad, the ant suggested, could swallow his anger.

"Swallow it?" asked the toad.

"Yes," said the ant. "It's possible. As long as you swallow it quickly, because it doesn't taste very nice."

"No," said the toad.

The toad could hide his anger so well that he'd never find it again.

Or he could let it drift out to sea and be calmed by the waves.

He could let his anger shrivel up until it disappeared.

Or he could sing it away.

"Sing it away?" asked the toad. "What do you mean?"

"Hmm, let's leave that one," said the ant. "It's possible, but it's hard to explain."

"Oh," said the toad.

The toad could give his anger away to someone who wanted to be really, really angry.

He could laugh it off.

The toad nodded. He liked that idea.

"No," said the ant, "probably better not do that one."

"Okay," said the toad.

He could squash it into a ball and kick it away.

He could paint it.

He could dance with it.

"Dance with anger?" asked the toad in surprise.

"Yes," said the ant. "Anger can't stand that. It withers away."

"Withers away . . ." said the toad thoughtfully, trying to imagine it.

He could nurse his anger.

"Nurse it?" asked the toad, wide-eyed.

"Yes, that's also possible. But let me finish," said the ant, sounding irritated.

"Go ahead," said the toad.

He could melt down his anger and let it evaporate.

He could chase it off.

He could think it away.

The ant stopped talking.

There was silence.

"What shall I do?" asked the toad, who was still angry.

"I'd throw it away," said the ant.

"Good thinking," said the toad, and he threw his anger away.

They shared some sweet dried nettles and talked about happiness, which, according to the ant, you never have to do anything about.

"You don't?" said the toad.

"No," said the ant.

THE BEETLE
AND THE CRICKET

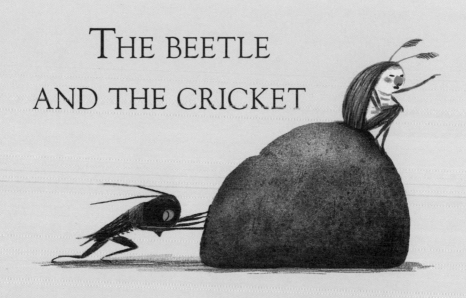

The beetle was explaining to the cricket how to get angry.

"No," he said, "don't close your eyes. Keep them open, but make them fierce. Like this." He narrowed his eyes.

"Ah," said the cricket. "Like that." He tried to do the same.

"Much better," said the beetle. He stepped closer. "And now, hunch yourself up to make yourself look menacing."

The cricket hunched.

"Fine," said the beetle. "You could look a little more menacing though. But that's not bad." He frowned and looked at the cricket. "The most important thing," he continued, "is to be genuinely angry. I mean, you have to have really angry thoughts."

"I don't have angry thoughts," said the cricket.
"I never do."

"Think of some, then," said the beetle. "It's not easy,
but it's possible."

The cricket tried to come up with some angry
thoughts.

He hunched over in a reasonably menacing way and
narrowed his eyes, but he couldn't think of any angry
thoughts.

"I've never had to do it before," he said eventually.

"What sort of things did you come up with, then?" the beetle asked.

"Well . . . honey, thistles, fine weather, things like that . . . I'm good at those." His eyes shone as he spoke.

The beetle sighed. "What a waste of time," he said.

"So, what do we do now?" asked the cricket.

"Pretend you're angry with me," said the beetle. "I've messed up your birthday, I've stood on your toes, bent your wings, told you how ugly you are and that you make a hideous racket . . . Start with that."

The cricket tried to hunch with greater effect, to make his eyes even fiercer, and he imagined the beetle tipping his birthday cake upside down, crushing his toes while dancing, and shouting for everyone to hear that he, the cricket, was making a hideous racket. "Hideous! *Hideous* . . ."

He felt a great anger building quietly inside him and suddenly he boxed the beetle's ears. "There!" he cried. "That's for you!"

The beetle fell backwards and lay waving his legs in the air.

"Well done!" he cried. "Well done, cricket!"

He had trouble getting back onto his feet.

The cricket had already forgotten his angry thoughts and he helped turn the beetle over.

"I'm sorry," he said, wide-eyed.

"You're sorry!" cried the beetle. "Sorry? 'Thank you, beetle.' That is what you should be saying. 'Thanks very much, beetle!'"

"Thank you, beetle," said the cricket.

The beetle nodded, indicating that the lesson was over.

The cricket nodded back, took a running leap, and flew away.

" 'Thank you, beetle!' " he heard the beetle calling after him. " 'Thanks very much!' "

"I'm very grateful, beetle," the cricket called back.

"So you should be!" yelled the beetle.

THE DAY NO
ONE WAS ANGRY

One fine day, all trace of anger disappeared.

It was summer.

The hippopotamus collided with the hedgehog, but neither of them got angry. The tortoise told the snail that he looked flustered, but the snail didn't mind. The ant ate the bear's cake, but the bear wasn't angry either.

The elephant wasn't angry with himself when he carelessly bumped into an oak tree and went sprawling with a great thud, and the frog wasn't angry when the heron tried to swallow him whole, yet again.

It was a very odd day.

Animals who hurt themselves by walking into things weren't angry. Those who felt sorry for themselves didn't say, "Pull yourself together!"

At midday, the animals met up in a clearing in the forest.

The cricket asked the elephant what he should feel if an elephant stepped on his toes while dancing: "Should I be thankful? Overjoyed?"

The elephant looked at him and shrugged.

"I don't know," he said. "Delighted, perhaps? Or astonished?"

No one seemed to know what to feel.

A little off to one side, the spider hung suspended between two stems of the rose bush. "I'm sad," she told them.

"Are you, spider?" said the hippopotamus. "And why not? You can be as sad as you like."

Dark clouds covered the sun.

"Let's gnash our teeth and stamp our feet," said the buffalo.

"Or have a spitting competition," said the weasel.

The animals tried gnashing, stamping, and spitting as far as they could, but they'd forgotten how.

They sat there gloomily.

The ant whispered in the squirrel's ear, "I fear the worst."

The squirrel nodded. He didn't know what the ant meant but he knew he was right.

Towards evening it grew cold and the animals huddled together.

Crossing his legs, the cricket accidentally kicked the rhinoceros's knee.

"Ouch!" cried the rhinoceros. "Watch out."

They were angry words.

Everyone looked at the rhinoceros in alarm. There was silence. Then everyone began to cheer. Anger was back.

The elephant slapped himself. "Ow!" he cried. "I needed that!"

And the beetle yelled furiously to no one in particular,
"Just you wait . . ."

Everyone went home promising themselves a good
bout of anger that night, for one reason or another.

"Do you still fear the worst?" the squirrel asked the ant
as they walked through the twilit forest.

"No," said the ant. "I'm still afraid of things . . ." He
frowned and looked up at the squirrel. "But I no longer
fear the worst."

The squirrel nodded, trying to come up with something
to get angry about, and asked no more questions.

TABLE OF CONTENTS

This edition first published in 2014 by Gecko Press, PO Box 9335, Marion Square, Wellington 6141, New Zealand • info@geckopress.com • English language edition © Gecko Press Ltd 2014 • All rights reserved • First American edition published in 2015 by Gecko Press USA, an imprint of Gecko Press Ltd • A catalogue record for this book is available from the National Library of New Zealand • Original title: *N'y a t-il personne pour se mettre en colère* © 2013, Albin Michel Jeunesse • Text by Toon Tellegen © 2002, Em. Querido's Uitgeverij B.V., Amsterdam • Illustrations by Marc Boutavant • Translated by Bill Nagelkerke • Edited by Penelope Todd • Typeset by Book Design Ltd, New Zealand • Cover design by Vida & Luke Kelly, New Zealand • Cover typefaces Mr. Happy and Mr. Lucky by Hipopotam Studio, Poland • Printed in China • ISBN hardback 978-1-927271-57-5 • ISBN paperback 978-1-927271-60-5

For more curiously good books, visit www.geckopress.com